Prunus Serotina

Peter Cherry

For adult literary consumption only.

"This is definitely for grown people."

Written: Peter Cherry
Audio performed: Peter Cherry
Illustration: Peter Cherry
Edited by Kalisha D. Lemmitt-Cherry
Angelic Reign, Inc. Publication
Copyright original print 2017;2023;2024
digital print 2017; 2023; 2024 and audio 2017; 2023
 by Peter Cherry and Angelic Reign, Inc.
ISBN: 9798990257849

Table of Contents

Beautiful

Gaze upon my moonlight sky.
Draped in night; shooting stars blazing bright.
Breezing through autumn leaves;
dancing with a cyclone; in mid-flight.
Thunderous bass; the band was thunder.
While the pulse from lighting's flash
mimics the first emotion of deep attraction;
the wind picks up the anticipation
of pleasure's pain within your sight;
creating a mist of teardrops on my shoulder;
intertwined in ecstasy; with an adamant erotic;
producing a psychological,
and sensual physical alchemist.
Perfecting the formula,
of Blue Flame.

Hey, Stranger

A somewhat stranger to my eyes;
I'm feeling you a little more than the same.
Genuine to my soul;
overthinking minds rationalize,
'Just another game.'
Mature by nature;
I'm a rock that can weather all types of storms.
Can be colder than ice;
just prefer to keep you warm.
Innocent by spirit; intended to never harm.
Other guys don't express much.
I guess I took a foot out of the box of the norm.
It's okay to be skeptical; still a stranger to your eyes.
She's pondering, "He wants to pursue me to the bed."
Truthfully;
that's only icing on a cake in which you've never fed.

Ladybug

I know I'm crazy.

It's just lately;

I've been within a mental drift;

about you and me taking slow walks in the park.

Cool as a breeze;

blowing trees; high off conversations that sparked.

You're delicate; strong; sexy; and smart.

Comfortable in your skin; the most beautiful art.

How long did it take to mistress

the craft of the heart?

To my soul, you are uplift.

A special kiss upon my lips.

Like the first breath

that released me from hell,

where I dwelled in an abyss.

Webster's dictionary describes you

as a spirit: courageous; lively; and bold.

I'm the spiritual principle in man.
I'm just an immortal soul.
Age is the only thing getting old.
You are my food when I hunger;
I'm your drink when you thirst.
Our passion intensifies naturally
because our communication works.
Now take off my shirt,
while I'm lifting up your skirt,
moving your panties to the side;
letting my tongue do all the work.
Licking you lady, making your leg shake.
As you climax in a squirt;
crème of the crop; I'm tasting every spot.
Until you damn near pass out, lovingly
cursing me out.

Call in the A.M.

It was 2:15 a.m.,

when I woke up after hearing the phone ring.

After the third ring,

I answered, "Hello?"

It was you on the other end saying,

"My body is throbbing."

I replied, "Who's this? Just playing..."

Then I replied, "Come over; I got what you need.

Leave it to me to produce a sexy scene."

You said, "I know what you mean.

Well, Boo; give me a few.

Better be ready for me;

because I'll start without you!"

I replied, "Yeah, me too."

Giggling, on the phone,

you replied, "Bye, fool."

3 a.m. came; I heard your knock.

As I opened the door,

I couldn't help but to give a modest roar,

"Sexy, you're looking hot!"

You replied, "Thank you, Boo… now shut up;
and come hit my spot!"
Tapping on walls, the sound of pleasure is heard
through walls and...why did I pause?
Really; it's only 1:15 a.m..
I was just having a dream!
I called you to come over to experience my scheme.

Dial Up

You can call me old-fashioned.

I'm not the one interested in having a cellular affair.

On my phone, you're sending naked pictures.

I would rather have your naked ass over here,

with your legs in the air.

We are both very busy people;

I understand communication is precious.

But, instead of texting me about today;

let's put some time aside for breakfast.

Now, I like social media;

you can search for my page, if you want to.

But I'm too old to be searching for you online,

or sending a friend message just to say.

"I want you."

I leave that for the younger ones; that's their style and all.

I'm a throwback, old-fashioned;

I just want to spend a little time, that's all.

Since this may seem out dated, and my input insufficient;

 I'm organic in time.

Vintage.

Worth way more than you can snap in an instant.

"Plugged"

For a week now,

I've been talking to this sexy ass chick online

by the name of Belle.

I met Belle surfing through a dating app.

We talked about how much we loved nature;

documentary stuff about lions and lionesses; dolphins and sharks.

You know; shit like that.

I'm a bit nerdy on the surface I admit, but damn it!

If she liked it, I loved it!

Well, on this particular night,

I'm being ran out of my office

because my 'mini fridge' keeps humming, and I can't concentrate.

I'm like, screw it!

I'll just sit on the couch in the lounge for

the remainder of my session.

I go into my delight as she sends me a message stating,

"Hey, Big Dick".

"I just wanted to know if you are plugged in?

We could chat a little better."

I messaged back, Belle,

"I'm all plugged in; just waiting for you."

Two minutes passed, and Belle types, "Talk to me."

Being the guy that I am, I respond back, "How about animals?"

The humming sound coming from my office gets louder.

Then she keys in, "I like all animals;

but I just truly love rabbits; at the moment."

I respond back like any man would,

and talk about exotic butterflies.

The humming noise in the background is getting to me.

Belle types back, "I attached some pics of me.

I hope you like them.

Sincerely, Belle."

She is fucking hot, I tell ya!

I hope that's her.

She has on a V-neck tee shirt, pulled down in the front

to show her nice, succulent breasts forming at the top.

The humming stops, then picks up again.

Every time I hear the humming in the office,

I respond to Belle.

It motivates me more to get closer to her.

Pulling out my phone, I start taking pictures,

so Belle can download them.

I rip off my tee shirt; show off my arms; and grab my crotch.

I send her all flex shots.

The next one she sends is a picture of her

eating an ice cream cone.

The way her tongue curves while licking it was priceless!

At this point, I can't take the humming sound anymore,

I jump off the couch and go down the hall to the second office.

I open the door, "I can't play this game anymore!"

A lady is bent over on the desk with a vibrator and laptop.

While still satisfying herself, she exclaims,

"Why'd you stop, Big Dick!?"

"I wanna join you!" I stand with my hard dick in my hand.

The lady leans up with a look of, "I'm gonna get you."

She walks towards me and hands me the vibrator.

"Finish me off then, Big Dick."

13

Falling to my knees, and position the vibrator to
follow behind my tongue.
She guides me to the floor, and sits on my face.
I throw the vibrator in the hallway.
I can tell she is making herself cum,
her clit's very sensitive.
I place my tongue on her delicate petals.
She has multiple orgasms.
She sits on my face for a while;
then arches her body enough to slide down
to my waist; and places me inside
of her extremely wet, tasty pussy.
She starts riding me.
I start humming to keep from cumming;
but the more I hum, the more she rides.
I can't hold it anymore!
She keeps going!
I'm about to blow!
Then I feel it; I'm about to cum!
I'm saying in my mind, "Four more movements."
On the third one, she gets off of me.
Surprised, I grab my dick;
my anticipation is apparent all over the place.
She kisses me; picks up the vibrator; and says,
"If you can't play right; I'll play by myself."

Interpersonal Freak

Interpersonally speaking,

common for using words for freaking.

"Don't look at your body?!"

"It's too gorgeous!"

"Believe me, I'm peeking.

Reaching for a condom,so I can just dig in deep.

Don't ask me to hit you raw.

Because whatever you got you keeping.

Save the conversation; after the fact,

I'll be sleeping.

Well, actually; after the fact,

I'll be leaving.

I haven't lied to you yet;

I'm a debatable heathen?

I would call you tomorrow;

but I can't think of a reason.

Boldly honest.

"You're wet?"

Because your inner thigh is leaking.

Talking Wild 2

"Come on, Suga!
Let's go in the backyard,
while this summer rain pours!"
"Why?"
"Shut up! Go outside, Sexy…"
"I'm gonna …Wait!"
"What? Woman,
 I will take off your dress
and eat through them thongs!"
"Why?"
"I'm horny!"
"Wait!"
"What's wrong?"
"Nothing!"
"You keep interrupting
 what I was trying to say!
Why wait!?!"

Comfy

Put your pleasant booty on my face.
I have my face go where your booty shake.
I stuck out my tongue;
and you tooted up, your clit I taste.
Mmmm so good; I made you uhhhhh.
As you drop down low, as you sit on my face.
Who am I to be so rude to say move,
as you invited my tongue all up in your place?
All of a sudden, your bottom did a dance;
with juices pouring from between your grace.
Drenched in your passion,
all that wetness draped down my face just for a taste.
Having you in a trance;
with your body swimming in outer space.

Besties

Twelve minutes ago,
Robin, an advertising executive,
who is dating a married man,
just got beat up by the guy's wife and some of her friends.
When the ladies returned early from a night out,
Robin got caught in an incriminating position
with the husband in bed.
Within moments of the mêlée,
Robin somehow manages to flee with just a torn
and stretched sundress.
She is leaving her lover at the mercy of the,
"kicking your ass;
STILL kicking your ass;
calling-your- momma-to-come-get-your-shit-
while-your-ass-still-yet-again-being-kicked" squad.
As Robin runs turning left down the end of the block,
two gunshots fire out.
Just knowing who those shots are meant for,
she runs down two more blocks; hitches a ride;
then walks four blocks to the home of her best friend, Rita.
Rita, an emergency room surgeon,
who is secretly sleeping with her boss;
is preparing to leave for the hospital,but is startled
by the frantic knocking and ringing of the doorbell
at 12:23 a.m. in a semi-quiet neighborhood.
"Robin?! What the hell?! Ooooh, bitch…
You slept with that mothafucka again didn't you!?"
Rita stares at Robin's scrimmage scars on her face and arms."
Damn!
You need to come on with me to the hospital!?"
Rita says in a rushing manner.

Waving her off, Robin says,"No---what? Stop girl!

This ain't shit; you should see them other bitches!"

As she sides steps away from being examined by Rita,

Robin replies,"I am not going to the hospital;

I'm too damn tired to move."

"You try running like a track star, barefoot,

trying not to step on glass or rocks!

My toenail polish is all fucked up!"

"Robin; get your stupid ass in the house!"

Rita opens the door wider so Robin can come in.

"Look heffa, you need to get yourself checked out.

You might have a concussion... your ass is already silly!

And, report what happened to you!"

"Besides, I'm on call and I gotta go."

"Rita! Girl, I can't do that.

Ummmm, nope; I can't do that one."

"Bitch! You are scaring me, okay!

I got to go I swear ..."

"Please! Go to work, save a life.

When you get back, girl,

I will tell you everything--- I won't budge.

I just need to get myself together.

I'm too damn rattled to talk to you..."

"Please, let me stay, please?" Robin begs.

"Ho; I can't believe or take you at

this present point and time, neither!

I don't have time to argue, or drag you into the car," says Rita.

"So, can I stay, bestie."
Robin says with a big smile.
"You can stay," Rita retorts with adding;
"At least I can identify your ass
when somebody's woman come snatch you."
"Aye; my lil' brother in the basement…"
"Girl, your brother twenty-two;
he ain't been lil in a while…"
trails off Robin.
Rita covering her ears says, "I'm not listening to you!!"
Rita lowers her hands down.
"He's working security; and leaving out soon."
Robin asks; "Where?"
"Good & Ugly; the club around the corner.
They chicken wings and burgers are the bomb.
Shit, the more you go to the club; it gives you party points,"
Rita says.
"What?!
You never wanted to go when I asked you before!"
exclaims Robin.
"Know what!
Whatever never mind, that's why you got beat up!" yells Rita.
Robin looks at Rita; "Don't be like that."
Rita continues, "I'll let him know on my way to work,
and not to bother you."
Rita walks down the hall to the basement door,
trying to get her brother's attention. Robin says,
" 'Good & Ugly'."
You gotta be thirty and up to be in there…"
Yelling up from the basement, Rita responds,
"He turns twenty-three next week;
the owner hired him to work the front door security!"
"What!" yells Robin, turning down the stereo from upstairs.
Throwing her hands up like,
'Whatever,' Robin walks down the hall
to continue the conversation.
"He got his security license three weeks ago, and working at,
Good & Ugly,"

Rita states in an annoyed manner,

walking back up from the basement stairs.

As Rita steps upstairs with sleep clothes in her arms,

she accidentally hits Robin with the door.

"Ahhh; damn! Haven't I been abused enough today!?

Shit!" Robin yammers sarcastically.

"My fault; damn."

Rita holds up her hands as to say, 'I surrender.'

I should be getting off later in the morning.

Hey; if shit don't look right, give me a call."

"Aight, Bighead; I shall!"

As she sits on the couch,

Robin presses the towel closer to her bruised face.

"Where's the remote?"

"The remote to activate everything is on the main speaker,"

says Rita. "Anyway; get some rest."

"Thanks, girl; you really are a cool friend."

"Where your face rags at?"

Getting and walking to the middle of the hall,

Robin looks in the mirror.

"Fuck! Look at my face!

I hate that bitch; I should've cut her ass…"

Slightly, she reflects, 'I shouldn't have been there…'

"It's okay, crazy,"

Rita replies, going into the linen closet and handing

her some towels.

"You know now; okay!?"

"You're right," says Robin.

"Call me, if you need me."

Rita says, rushing and looking for her other shoe. "

I'll be cool; just be safe driving to work."

Rita grabs her purse, and leaves out the door.
Robin blows her a kiss,
then proceeds to the bathroom to clean her wounds.
About ten minutes later,
slightly wet from her shower,
she exits the bathroom, and walks towards the stairs.
She smells the aroma of marijuana and incense.
Slowly, she opens the door.
She walks downstairs,
drapes the towel over her left shoulder,
and finds Rita's little brother smoking
and cussing at the video game.
Smiling, she makes her way towards him.
"Hey!"
Startled by nakedness; Jimmy jumps up,
"What the fuck!"
"What do you think you doing?" ask Robin,
drying herself; leaving nothing to the imagination.
Repositing her towel to cover up
the front side of her body,
Robin asks Jimmy,
"Does your sista know what you're doing?"
Stuttering,
and looking intense,
he speaks, "I...I... I... shit! I what?"
She starts walking closer.
"I tell you what; give me a hit of that;
and it will be our lil secret, okay?"
Passing the blunt to Robin,
he says, "I've been smoking."

She reaches out for the smoke.
"I thought you had to be at work?"
"It's slow, the club owners texted
me to come in tomorrow."
Passing it back after she took a drag.
"Could you be a dear and go get me the lotion?"
"Sure, I can do that for you."
"Wait a minute; what am I doing?" asks Jimmy.
"Lotion. Are you gonna get it?
Or, you just gonna keep looking at my tits?"
As he goes up the stairs with much haste,
Jimmy grins with mild embarrassment.
"Ah, yeah."
He smiles like Christmas came in July.
While shaking her head,
Robin takes strong puffs off the blunt;
knowing she gave Rita's brother mega wood.
"What kind of phone he got?"
She grabs and starts looking through his phone,
and saw the text: 'Since you couldn't hear me!
I'm about to go to work, and my girl,
Robin is here; she's spending the night.'
 "Hmm…" Placing the phone back how she saw it,
Robin looks across the room and sees a CD player.
"How y'all still got CDs.."
She picks up the classic CDs, and glances until
she finds what she was looking for.
"Oooh; the second CD!"
 She puts it in the CD player, and hits the third song.
"Oooh; this my shit!" Seductively, she dances; puffing
the blunt even harder.

Jimmy comes down the stairs with the lotion.
"Here you go."
Walking towards him with a sexy bounce in her step,
she kisses him on the cheek.
"Thank you, Jim."
Gently she touches his hand, removing the lotion.
Robin goes to the edge of the couch,
placing her left leg up,
slowly moisturizing from her toes all
the way up to her inner thigh.
Jimmy just looks with a blank stare,
not knowing if he should say something,
go for broke, go upstairs, or go play with himself.
As she proceeds to the next limb,
she turns over to her young audience and replies;
"You finished hitting this?"
"Huh? Aw; I mean no," says Jim.
"Well, come over here and talk to me."
Walking towards her naked silhouette near the TV,
he gently takes the blunt out of her mouth.
With a nervous shake
on her way to her destination, the couch,
Robin takes her lotion-free hand and rubs
the crotch of Jimmy's sweatpants.
Stretched out like a diving board, and premature
in all the circumstances at this point,

he seats himself at the far edge of the couch.

"I don't bite; unless, that's what you want,"

she says, grinning with a naughty intent.

"What? Come on now;

I'm around naked chicks all day long.

I'm dat dude; plus you cool with my sis."

"Okay…Dude, could you do another favor for me then?"

Hastily Jimmy asks, "What?"

"Lotion my back, please,"

Robin states, in a demanding; sultry manner.

She places herself on the other end of the couch.

Jimmy slides over to Robin, catching a side view of her face.

"What happened to you?"

"Nothing really… I just got into it with a bitch."

"It must have been a big bitch."

Sarcastically, Robin laughs.

"Oh; you got jokes?"

Jimmy rebutts,

"I'm just saying; it looks like you were in a prizefight ..."

"Enough; already!

You got a tank top, jersey, or something?"

Shaking his head, he states,

"Revere didn't do all that shit for you."

Robin is looking at him like he

about to fuck up the church's money, "You're okay.

I just don't want to venture there right now!"

Robin exclaims.

Jimmy walks towards the dryer, getting a tee shirt.

He walks back to the couch,

with the preverbal foot-in-the-mouth. "Here you go."

"Thank you.

Hey; I didn't mean to snap on you; forgive me."

She bats her eyelashes in a silly manner.

"Tell you what;

let me beat your ass playing the game, okay?"

As he gets up to grab the controllers,

Robin grabs Jimmy's arm, pulling him closer to her.

"Not those; these controllers."

For the night,

Robin is replacing the married man with Jimmy.

Like That

It's something about ...

When you cross my path;

it's like a breath has been taken from me.

Eloquently speaking.

When I talk to you,

it's like you're listening to The Isleys'

taking the "Voyage to Atlantis."

My enchantress.

As I look in your eyes,

it's like watching a star shine so bright within the darkest of

night. When I touch your heart,

it's like feeling the calm of, "Peace on earth."

Right.

When making love,

it's like the sun intensifies our heat;

while the wind cools us down, with the help from our sweat.

I bet.

As I slowly venture down;

anointing your body with kisses;

it's like I must insist to...

Like This

It's something about the way ......

"Hold up; and wait a minute.
Didn't you tell me
that you wanted me to trim it?!
Meet me in the bathroom in two minutes."
Moments sharing; having fun; being intimate.
"Uh, this I like."
Eloquently speaking.
Turning your body to the side,
I move your panties to the side;
as we gaze upon each other's eyes.
Your body's throbbing;
as you're placing me inside.
Spread your legs to the sky;
unless you want to be in the tub.
Then, relax one leg to the side.
This I like; when we're talking.
This I like; when we're listening.
This I like; to our hearts.
This I like.
When making love; this I like.

Using rose and lavender; ready to lather you.
Oooo! It's blowing kisses at me!
Slip me your tongue,
it's like a breath has been taken from me.
Anointing your body with kisses,
it's like the sun intensifies our heat.
I slowly venture down on you…

It's like I must insist to…

-Hey-

Damn Good

Damn; what a nice night.

I wasn't expecting such generosity,

just for taking her to a concert, and grabbing a bite.

As her aura paints her silhouette by the moonlight;

tongue lashes are placed upon her pussy;

reciting love under her water;

profound by the depth of the orgasm especially thrice,

she's rubbing the top of my head,

telling me she wants to give some love back.

Moving to a comfortable position that she likes;

proceeding to speak into the mic.

I don't know what I did to entice.

All I know is that I gave her a pat on the back,

holding her arm up, because she swallowed,

and said it went down the wrong pipe.

I felt it was only polite;
we're in a sixty-nine position,
my tongue was going la, la, la;
she started moving her pussy across my tongue;
while she kept on sucking my dick
like we're in a competition.
I can't predict who's going to win.
Damn, she got me floating.
It looks like there is no tap out in sight.
We started at 11:50 p.m.
By 12:05 a.m., I was taking laps in her ocean.
Backstroking; doggy paddling;
swimming in the deep end.
Deep in---deep, deep in.
Then back to shallow, while the tip's in.

Listen

Allow me to paint you this picture of,
'Sexy.'
I will turn into sensual.
Be your love animal;
prey upon you;
and get you.
I will start off by feeding you
fruits of enlightenment; comedy;
and misbehaving.
As you're full,
 navigate my hand to a forbidden place.
If you want me to stop, just say,
"Wait!"
Aw; too late!
Instead of being the hunter,
I'm the prey?!
Your mission was to stay and play.
As you unbutton my shirt,
I'm taking off your skirt.
In this game of passion,
we are proving more than just flirts;
engaging in sexy positions.

"Casting Couch"

After answering the phone,
a voice projects from a dark corner
of the room saying, "Okay; lighting looks good!
We are gonna do a fade-in with the camera.
I want the framing to be perfect to open up with…
wait a minute."
A phone rings; he answers the phone.
"Hello! What?! How long you gonna be?!
If you would have taken the route,
I gave you you wouldn't be stuck in rush hour!"
"Do you know how many people showed up just to audition?!
So, today we got an excellent B roll shoot for however long..."
"And we did that yesterday," says the Director.
"Okay, okay, okay!
Everything's cool!
Get here safe. Bye!"
"Listen up, everyone!
I guess you all heard?!" he yells.
"Never hire your baby's momma
just to get out of paying child support!"
"By the way; love those track shots last night.
 My crew rocks!" The Director calls, "Next!"
A lady walks in.
"Okay; thumbs up! Babe, are you ready?
Not you, madam," states Director.
" Babe is the camera person.
Now everybody shut the fuck up,we checking the audio".
"In 3, 2, 1."

The audio is checked, the camera fades-in then slowly pans,
with a close up from the feet of a lady
wearing alligator gladiator sandals.
The lady sits on the half-chaise.
Seductively, she crosses her legs.
She is modeling a black chemise with a mid-rise lace thong.
The Director says, "Ummm! My, my, my!
You look absolutely tasty;
and smell so delicious!"
"Not you, madam; catering just brought a pie."
"What's your name, Darling?"
He asks, and looks at the lady on the half-chaise.
"I'm actually calling you 'Darling'
because I'm old; not to offend anyway,"
continues the Director's voice from the dark corner of the room.
With a seductive, nonchalant stare,
she looks into the camera, smiles and says,
"My name is Berda.
I'm a forty-two-year-old retired police officer.
I left for these reasons: I was completely burned out;
the pay sucked;
and doing this makes twice what I made on the force.
I had little to no social life; no time for me."
"Oh!" exclaims the Director.
Giving a slightly glazed look towards the voice in the corner,
Berda looks in the camera; winks and says,
"I have a story to tell."
"After I left the force, dating was tough.
 I constantly stayed on guard like I was still on duty."
"Until one day,
I fell for this photographer, and dating him was a dream!
Our conversations were refreshing:
ranging from social; political; art; and fashion."

"Mentally, I was on cloud nine.
But physically…"
"Go on," prompts the Director.
"I thought I wasn't attractive enough.
I didn't know if he had another woman until
I caught him in my yellow sundress,
giving himself a manicure!
I didn't know what to do;
I was frozen with shock!"
"Then after the shock wore off, I got mad.
Then I thought, 'Okay; it's time to let you have it!'"
"Instead, I giggled and said,
'Quit stretching my shit, bitch!'"
He was so caught off guard
he spilled my five-dollar nail polish!"
"I admit; knowing that was a sigh of relief!
Then it turned slightly awkward.
I stayed with him for a little while."
"Sometimes, we'd hang out and talk about messy shit."
"Look, I didn't want to start another relationship;
what did you expect?"
Motioning with a sympathetic pout, she purrs,
"What?!
He was so gorgeous; I had to try.
After eleven months, I broke up with him.
It may seem messed up on my part
But…Berda got to have her sugar melted."

"I will go for a walk wearing velour with no panties on…
if you do it right you, can get a little orgasm!
Not all women know how to work that muscle,
but I can," she says, smiling and motioning to the camera,
"Oh; I wasn't supposed to say that?
Fuck it then!" she laughs.
"Anyway."
"I would walk in his neighborhood,
and one particular day, sort of mid-evening,
I was walking and heard the sounds of multiple moans.
Being an ex-cop, I went to investigate.
As I got closer to where the sounds were deriving from,
I noticed it was coming from two locations.
I proceeded to the first house.
In the front window,
without any curtain or shade to hide behind,
I saw this interracial couple, possible newlyweds;
setting up a web camera,
and moving some furniture around
in the middle of their living room."
"Subconsciously curious, I wanted to stay.
I placed myself out of view and watched.
After they got everything prepared like they wanted,
the groom picked up his wife
and placed her in the middle of this cute,
leather, four-piece sectional sofa.

With his hands gesturing to her, he starts filming."
"She's lowering the straps of her lace bridal gown,
caressing her body as if she was gonna explode,
all while licking her tongue out for a kiss.
The handsome groom tilted the camera
and looked at their computer...
I guess to see if the angle was right.
Then he began kissing the drape of her neck,
inching his hands slowly; venturing down her wedding lace."
"The way she responded; he must had found
that spot that just make you wanna do thangs!"
"By this time, I couldn't help but to play with my nipples."
"The more I needed to leave, the more I had to stay."
"As the groom gently placed his head
to anoint the lips of their union,
I drew closer to the window.
By the way he had her positioned;
I could see the lashing of his tongue across her lips."
"She started off rubbing his head across her pussy;
then drew him in closer.
I knew she had to tell him to place that tongue deep."
"Let me tell it, because she started moving her hips
like he was inflating a water balloon filled with juice!
She was screaming out, 'All over your face, Big Daddy!'"
"At this point, I'm rubbing on my nipples,
and rubbing my thighs."

"While touching my nipples;
I hear shots ring out from a second location!"
"I'm like, 'Oh, shit!'"
"I turned towards that direction,
but then came back to see if I could still see anything."
"Well, did you?" asks the Director.
"Fuck yes I did!"
"Look…I know, I was tripping out, but I didn't care.
I kept watching as she creamed all on that man's face!
Erect like a lollipop; I guess he found out
how many licks it takes to get to the center of that pussy."
As she continues to tell the story,
Berda starts laughing and playing with herself.
"Pardon me," she says after she takes her middle finger
out of her mouth.
"The whole look was so fucking erotic,
I just wanted to join in!"
"Horny as hell, I was playing with myself,
until heard a car coming; so I quickly left."
After closely listening, the Director starts
clearing his throat and begins to speak.
"Damn! A sexy, ex-cop looking for pleasure
to the point of being criminal!"
"So…you a freak like that?"
"I like it! Please continue."
Berda responds, "Well, walking back,
I felt embarrassed and a little paranoid about what I did.
The closer I walked back to his place,
my feelings started to change.
I started laughing at myself."
"By the time I inside his door,
I started thinking about what I saw.

I found my fingers rubbing against my clit.
My mind made me sex myself to the point of orgasm!"
"I made my pussy squirt, actually surprising myself!"
"I know I have a crème center but,
I didn't know I could do that!"
"Damn, Officer Berda!
I could just imagine you with
a flashlight and handcuffs,"
says the Director from the dark corner.
Berda draws closer to the camera
and responds in a seductive, nonchalant demeanor.
"Officer Berda!?
No, suga; that was a lifetime level ago!"
"My name is Bubbles by Berda."
"Besides;
I never found being in handcuffs sexy, except that one time…"
A phone rings from the distant corner.
"Cut!" grumbles the Director.
"Yes, yea… ten minutes, okay?! We will be here."
"Berda, love you; love your story!"
"Thank you for sitting in; we were able
to get the lighting and everything perfect.
Our stars are on their way; but I want to hear more."
"Can you stick around so we can hear some more of your stories?"
The camera dissolves back in a slight angle on
a preoccupied Berda,
now checking herself out in a handheld vanity mirror.
The Director from the dark corner of the room says,
"I just have to ask my favorite Berda a question."
Moving the vanity, and moving to show more of her figure
to the camera, she purrs.

"Please; ask away."

The voice continues, "

Was that your first time being 'a peeper'?"

Rubbing her hands together, "To that extreme, no.

There was one time I saw a couple by

accident,and it was a bit wild."

With interest, the Director asks, "What happened?"

Berda looks in the camera with a look of,

'I'm glad you asked.'

"Never told anybody this, but when I was on the force,

I was watching store surveillance footage on a case of

smash and grabs."

"Well... the owners of this particular...,"

Berda says, clearing her throat,

"You have to officially interview me for that."

Cheese Cake

Tastes like chocolate strawberries;

detecting the aroma of passionate cherry, and grape.

While you're sipping on a word potion,

with me as the chase.

I can be intoxicating when you swallow

the sweetest thing; peaches and crème.

Open now;taste the love from my fingertips; in return,

I'll taste the pear from your lips; juicy.

My hunger calls me to be creative with

whipped crème; caramel; milk bath; and butterscotch;

on a curved apple bottom canvas.

Painting ice cream castles with hilltops made of gum drops.

Enjoying my lollipop.

The scenery is getting hot; melting sugar rolls

down from in between.

I place a single gesture of ice;slowly melting from my tongue.

Feeling desires heat deep within your ocean;

bathing in nectar.

Honey

I got off work.
I cooked dinner.
I took the trash out.
I put the kids to bed at nine.
Now, you're about to put me to work?
Your feet were hurting.
I rubbed your feet.
Starting from the ankles, and drifting up to your hips.
You are verbally talking to me,
while I want to tongue kiss your lips.
Panties off, or to the side?
The sheer vanity of you neglecting my erection is not fair
Place your titty in my mouth, or something damn it!
Hunching better than a porno picture.
Giving you a whole lot of tongue;
about to give you all of this **DICK!**
My stroke's making you loud and shit.
I don't want to wake the kids up!
She told me to shut up and slapped me with her titties.
Oh, damn!

She even gave me some.

It was good!

Oh, shit!

Hopefully, they didn't hear me.

Put that freaky juice on me.

"Ten Minutes"

It is ten minutes after midnight, and...
I'm on my way home after being at the club.
This is early for me.
Normally, I get home much later.
I know what you're thinking.
That's messed up, and there's nothing out there in those places.
You bet my Lady just hates it.
Well, it's kind of funny; really!
That's where I met my beloved.
We always frequented this hole-in-the-wall club.
That where we're regulars.
Hell.
My old high school love is now co-owner and DJ of the place!
Yes.
I helped a little.
What is that I hear you're saying?
Wait, let me guess,
"You're getting involved with an ex-love and you have a lady?"
"Not smart!"
Please; don't judge or hate me for making money
and pulling strings;that's what I do!
I'm a concert promoter; and, ironically,
it's coming close to us being together five years.
Wow, that's it; my epiphany.
If she is not here, why am I?
Now don't get me wrong;
my Lady never disapproves of me going to the club by myself.
Lately, she hasn't been having a desire to go.
However,
she never gets mad at me for going and coming in around 3 a.m
Shit.
Together we close the club down and hit up a diner,
we normally get home at 7 a.m.
I figured too much clubbing can make you cool on going for a
Like any good man, I held it down for the both of us.

I pull out my phone, and I am going to call my
Lady and tell her I am coming home.
Then I hear the sweetest sound.
"Here is your vodka and cranberry."
"Thank you, Cheyenne," I reply, tipping her five dollars.
"You got a minute?
You seem like you were in deep concentration," she asks.
"No; just daydreaming...I say.
"About?" she asks.
"Nothing...what's up?" I ask.
"Well, I know you're fifth anniversary is coming up,
and I was wondering if you have anything planned?"
"Damn, Cheyenne!"
"Not trying to pry; just wanted to help in any way," she blushes. "
I don't mean to sound like I'm snapping at you; my apologies,"
I say picking up my drink.
"You're fine; I'm getting in your business..."
she says as she turns.
Before she starts to walk away, I reply, "Cheyenne;
I'm glad you asked." "What would be nice to do?"
She walks up to me and gives me a modest peck on my lips. With a
mischievous smirk she replies, "Surprise her."
Looking at her with bewilderment, I say in my cool way,
"Damn, Cheyenne!" Smiling, she says, "I got to get back to work.
Enjoy your drink. Shit, I would just surprise her."
Cheyenne always liked to hustle with me.
She works with me on the side,
finding the hottest local or national talents.
When musicians come through,
her coming over to our house and partying wasn't nothing.
She is pretty much a professional socialite.
I listen to a few songs, just enough to finish my drink.
I place a tip on the table, and then head out to my car.
I stop at a twenty-four-hour grocery; get some flowers;
a bottle of liquor; and some scratch-offs.

Let me tell you,
I am ready for my baby!
On the way to the car,
I pick up a heads-up dime off the ground, jump in the car,
and head for home.
As I pull up to the house,
I use the dime to scratch off one of the tickets.
I won $200.00! Shit, this gon be a NIGHT!
I start undressing from the car.
Without dropping the bag with the liquor and flowers,
I pull off my shirt and shoes.
Quickly, I unlock the door and disarm the alarm,
trying not to wake her up. Getting butt ass naked
with gifts of sexual romance in my hands,
I walk upstairs to our room.
The door is halfway open.
I hear a far too familiar sound; the one of pleasure!
I have bestowed this upon my Lady's lower lips many times before
My body is overwhelmed with many degrees of temperatures.
I move forward in haste.
I see her, wearing my favorite tee shirt.
My Lady of deceit; but no less, my Lady.
I know now why she had stopped fancying the club!
Grasping the sheets… is this a …woman?!
Sensually, she is kissing between my Lady's soft legs,
tasting her sweet juices. I want to yell, "
I'm the one who trimmed that bush, Vixen!"
Yet, I cannot utter a sound.
I want to move forward and express my disappointment,
but my body couldn't…wouldn't allow me
to respond in a timely manner.
It is like I am stuck in a time warp of heartache.
Seductively, they move as still as snapshots to pixels,
and then speed up to slow motion.
The only thing I can do is watch.
That's when I start to get aroused.

This mysterious; beautiful; and voluptuous lady
is wearing a blue bustier and crotchless stockings.
Her hair, along with the moon and mood lighting
of our bedroom, places a silhouette of shadow on the wall.
It covers her face.
The only twinkle of light shimmers from her tongue ring;
as she slowly licks my beloved Lady's clitoris,
making her quiver with liquid emotion.
Look at them so delectable; horrible;
and erotic heart-achingly beautiful.
I start to wonder if they are even aware of me.
Ecstasy blankets my anger,
and it transforms into a fantastic feeling.
My own existence at this time is to view the show.
I call out, "Puddles!"
Frozen within intrigue of this sight.
This mysterious love in lace is making my
beloved wet up my tee shirt.
She is curving her tongue in a manner of scooping
from the bottom of the taint, to the top of the clitoris;
just licking up and down towards
the center of my lady's precious pearl.
Vixen's pearled tongue dips into the
creaminess of my lovely. I cum.
I curse you!
Intoxicating Vixen; drunk off of my special reserve's love!
Filled with a mouthful of my beloved's nectar
from her creamy regions, where I make my home! Vixen.
How dare you instantly get me aroused again!
As I marvel in their mystery,
they seem to keep up with the body movements.
While she is sampling my beloved,
they appear to have an orgasm.
Just look at them; just in their own existence!
I can't believe that mysterious Vixen!
How dare her cum,
while breaking my heart with every slow lick!?
I gaze upon her hand movements,
as she slowly rubs her clit... wait a minute;

What is that I see on her left cheek!?
While the Vixen licks and slowly plays with herself,
I wish to be those sheets for just a few moments.
She begins to drip puddles.
Wait a minute; I notice the birthmark for the second time.
There is something very familiar about her birthmark.
Now, I've seen this birthmark before.
Don't get me wrong;
I've been around the block a couple times, but I'm not a ho!
Where have I seen this before?
The only one I remember...no, it couldn't be?!
The only person that I knew with a birthmark
on her left rear was my old high school girlfriend.
What the fuck?!
Thoughts of going skating; to the movies;
prom; holding her hands; and even the first time we kissed, run
through my mind.
For a brief moment, I feel as if my own chicks invaded my past!
Slowly, past times begin to catch up with reality.
My body begins to show signs of movement.
In reverse, I lean back in the hallway.
My hand cramps.
Finally, the feeling goes back into my hand,
as I set down my gifts for tonight. I should just leave; walk out.
Shit!
My interest has become an investment to see this till the end.
Upset and aroused to perfection, I must continue.
As I lean forward to observe a bit closer,

I accidentally knock over some lotion on the hardwood floor.
This startles both ladies.
"Oh! My goodness!"
"What the fuck!?"
"How long have you been standing there?!
With so many thoughts of things I could say
circling through my head,
I want to reply, "Awwwww!
I caught you, bitch! It's over!
I wanna participate in this right here!
Now move over!"
The only thing I can mutter is,
"What did you do with my Lady?!"
I can't think of shit to say!
My Lady shouts, "Baby!"
With an equal tone, Vixen shouts, "Boopy!"
I respond, "How could the both of you do me this way?!
I never loved this hard before.
I feel like both of you cheated on me.
Y'all know me more than anyone!"
While I'm expressing my pain; my hurt;
I forget that I am completely naked with---
a perfect erection I may add---and my ex-girlfriend,
Vixen, and my Lady, are fixated on the motions of my dick.
"What the fuck?!"
My old love, Vixen interrupts my howls, raising her hand,
"We are having a business meeting."
Both of them are giggling like I'm a joke.
"What the fuck?!," I say again.
My Lady is playing with herself in the mist of this moment.
Then she replies,
"Well, you always said that her head game was the best;
so I had to find out for myself."

"Thank you so much!" Vixen says smiling.
"Why don't you get on the bed and catch the second show?"
states Vixen. "Only one rule," says my Lady.

"You can't touch us; but we can touch you."

Dammit, woman!

What do you want from me?!

I caught my Lady, and my Vixen from the past,

anointing the place where I lay my head?!?

At that moment, both of them say almost in complete unison,

"You've been in love with two women for too long,

and we love you..." Time stood still.

What's more, did Cheyenne know all along,

and send me here to catch them in the act, or for me face the truth?

I love them both equally for so many different reasons and ways.

Then time corrects itself again...

"So, shut up and enjoy the show, or go to another room!"

"What the hell?!"

I say with a smile, rethinking my role in this scene.

"I'm staying! I'm a grown man; ya'll can't tell me..."

Both are kissing me around my neck.

I know; ya'll can call me a bitch-ass SUCKA for all I care!

All I know is my Beloved Lady is grasping on my dick,

while Vixen feels on my thighs, and starts to kiss Lady's soft lips.

So, I sit here on the bed with the women I adore as a willing prop…

Chill'n Wit U

Sexy you, sweet you.

It's your mind; heart; smile; lips; ass; and them tits.

Fuck... all of it!

I've just prepared some libations.

The cups are chilled to freak perfection.

As you're putting rollers in your hair,

I'm sitting here in this chair, having an erection.

Looking at your sexy body, I want some affection.

Bring your naughty self to me.

Straddle me you nasty whore.

Kiss me on my neck; place my dick inside of you.

I'll let you choose where.

Kiss and lick on my earlobe real slow,

move your hips like you are listening to your favorite song.

Kiss my lips.

Place more of my dick inside of you.

Throw it back; you can take it.

You are wetter than water.

Kiss me.

That tasty pussy; freaky ass delicious; so gushy that pussy.

I don't give a damn if it's trimmed or if it's bushy.

I love you.

You like it.

Intoxicating

I never knew such a thirst,

until I've sipped upon your lips.

Moist and pabulum as honeydew,

on a sunny spring morning.

The taste of your tongue is sweet like sugar.

I need some water to help dissolve this feeling.

"I can't deny."

Beauty is the vision;

while the sight of your smile and hips

beckon me to have another sip.

"I need some cognac."

While I'm wondering,

"How long will this addiction last?"

You keep me feeling high, when I look in your eyes.

For every man, you're a prize.

"So, what am I to do?"

"Should I drink upon you until I turn blue?"

Instead, I'll sober up a bit and show you what I can do.

Perhaps that way, you may feel intoxicated, too.

Kiss Yourself

When was the last time
you placed your fingertips on your nipples,
slowly massaging until you started
feeling your response to yourself?
Out of curiosity,
as you stimulate your areoles,
does it tingle like a blissful kiss;
or do you feel the warmth traveling down south;
like sunrays during a beautiful spring afternoon?
Just imagine slowly guiding your hands
down your stomach, and with your ring finger
slightly tickling your belly button.
Venture further.
Touch-it.
Then-kiss-yourself.
Then-kiss-me.
Kiss-yourself.
Kiss-me.
Kiss-yourself.
Kiss-me.
Touch-me.
Feel-me.
Taste-me.
Take-me.
You got my legs shaking;

I feel the softness of your tits.
Take me out, give it a kiss.
I like the taste of you.
You like the taste of me?
There is a place on my face
that can make you blush.
Would you like a seat?
Lick.
Delicious.
Lick.
Tongue kissing your clitoris.
Riding my face; moaning.
Drench me in your bliss.
I'm asking for it.
Kiss-yourself.
Kiss-me.
Kiss-yourself.
Kiss-me.
Touch-me.
Feel-me.

"The Gallery"

Starting off …
I was looking at this website called the,
' La Pooh Bougie Art Gallery.'
I have never seen so many beautiful rare exhibits before.
Then I noticed there was a contest for their private collection,
'Le Sexe Dans Mouvement' (Sex in Movement) exhibit.
It was the 99th year anniversary.
A five-day, all-inclusive expense paid trip.
Only two invitations were to be given in a raffle.
Not thinking too much of it.
I signed up and entered.
After my 11:20 a.m. meeting, I checked my email.
I won a ticket! Like, Oh, shi! I'm doing my happy dance.
The exhibits had caught my eye,
but I didn't think I was going to win!
That's like a one in a million chance; I know, right!
Anyway, I wanted to tell somebody about my luck.
I caught one of the interns before she got on the elevator.
I was like; "Mandi! Hey; can I catch a ride with you?"
Holding the elevator doors, she replied,"Sure Miss Lucky; come on."
Because I don't like half of the people I work with,
I started telling her about it.
"Hey, can I ask you something?
Which type of outfit would look good for the 'LaPooh Gallery...?'"
Before I could finish my sentence, Mandi verbally spewed,
"Wouldn't have taken you for the artsy type." '
Jealous little nugget!' I retorted in my mind instantly.
Putting my hands on my hips, with my eyes I look upon,
"It's all about intellectual, sexy chic."
"No disrespect; if I may?" Mandi asked.
I responded please give me your opinion.
"I didn't think that would be your cup of milk."

I asked myself, 'Who hired her again?'
The elevator door opened to Mandi's floor.
Mandi said, "I attended a few; it's art;
music; leather; and literature."
She stepped off the elevator.
As the doors shut, I lose my look of attitude
and shape it to more of curiosity.
I replied, "Intellectual; sexy; chic,"
"Yeah!"
On the way back to my office, I walked by a sheet of metal.
My reflections showed a truth I never faced before.
That crazy heifer's hip phrase left me haunted.
I know I had the intellectual part down without a problem;
I had always been secure with myself...yet...
Looking at my present outfit, 'sexy' was 'nil';
a black broomstick skirt; chunky, sandals;
and colorful kittens T-shirts.
I look more like a lonely cat lady,
moonlighted as a scrapbooker, and proud of it!
Still, this notion bothered me so much.
In fact, when I left work,
I found myself calling my cousin,Tiffany.
Tiffany had always been a fun, wild freak-of-the week genius.
Actually,in addition to a partial scholarship,
she became a stripper to pay part of her way through college.
She got a Master's Degree in Business Administration,
married a great guy with two kids;
and owned a lingerie and sex toy store near her shoe store.
I drove over to her place.
Looks like she doing some renovations.
As I looked at this guy's ass crack, I headed
out the door and walk towards my cousin's shop.
Seeing me through the shop window,
I heard Tiff tell her employee to close the shop.
As I entered, she walked over and hugs me.
"Hey, Cuzin!

It's been awhile!
Come on, let's go to the back.
I added a coffee and smoothie bar."
Going back there, I started telling her what transpired.
As she got a bit heavy handed pouring the rum in the blender,
Tiff chuckled.
"When did you start caring about if you look sexy or not?
You don't even take selfies."
"Gee; thanks, Tiff."
"Now, don't get me wrong;
you have always been the dependable; reliable; serious;
the smart one…"
I interrupted and said,
"That's my point…"
"I'm the sensible, one!
Never the charismatic one;
I've never done anything wild!"
My sex life is virtually nonexistent, my last couple of dates were
so boring I would have been more
entertained watching a pothole being filled!"
"I cannot remember the last time I truly let my hair down,
I went out and explored, hell didn't even drink really until now."
"Fuck it! Oooh that drinks mines thank you …"
I grabbed a drink. "Wait a minute, I can..."
Tiff reclaimed the conversation.
"It was New Year's Eve, 2003.
You got drunk off of Aunty May's rum balls."
She smirked and poured herself a glass.
"See; that's what I'm saying; rum balls!"
Handing me a different flavored daiquiri, Tiff said, "Girl!
We're cute and fine!"
"Look, I'm going to close the shop early anyway to do inventory.
Besides people shop online 24/7; everyday a celebration.
Aye lil cousin why don't you keep taking sips of my world famous,
"Lick Me" flavored daiquiri...
that will be in liquor stores in two months!
Let your big cousin help you pick out a few things."
What could I say but alright?!
Tiffany is the only one I know who can party,
and make money at the same time!

While trying on different outfits in the dressing room,
I kept looking at myself in the mirror, posing,
attempting to make seductive facial expressions.
I felt silly.
"Maybe I'm thinking too much about it.
Maybe I shouldn't go."
Instantly, the curtain pulled back.
Tiff had another outfit.
"Don't talk like that!
"Besides me with some sense, you're the only one in the family!"
She looks in the mirror at herself a bit.
"Luci!"
"Luci goosy! Look at you!"
"Girl, your body looks almost better than mine."
"Damn near competition; but my booty's bigger."
We both laughed, and I gave her a hug.
Her employee walked by; see us hugging, and looked.
Tiff turned to her employee and said,
"If I let you take a picture, that's twenty dollars!"
Her employee giggled and walked off.
"You got to go for yourself and have the time of your life!"
"You may even run into 'Mr. Right Now.'
And besides; it's free, girl!"
Time passed, and before I knew it,
I was at the airport, then on the plane.
I arrived at the next airport.
At the luggage claim was a cute guy with an almond complexion,
who held a, 'LaPooh Gallery' sign with my name,
and a, "Ferna Jo" or, "Fern Jo" name on it.
He was looking and standing around until I got his attention.
Saying, " 'LaPooh Gallery'; over here!" cute face walked up to me.
As he approached closer; for some reason,
I kept on staring at his crotch.
"Excuse me, miss, for being a little late."
"Our other winner's flight arrived early,
and she was very adamant about getting to the room... her... room."

"I'm your driver Reggie..."
Thinking in my head, 'I'm a Capricorn... Damn...'
"...from the art gallery; and congratulations on being a winner."
"Thank you," I replied. My luggage appeared.
"Oh, here I am.
As my polka dot suitcases turned in the carousel,
we both leaned over to grab it.
We touched hands, and within that brief second,
I took a whiff.
Damn, he smelled so good!
I started to act fake towards him...
Don't ask me why I placed that type of energy on him
because I could not answer my own self.
"I can get my own bags, thanks!"
"Miss, are you sure it wouldn't be a problem?"
"No! I'm fine just...rather do it myself."
He looked at me like he just missed something.
"Okay," Reggie replied, as he led me to the car.
While we walked to the car,
Reggie asked with a non-threaten sarcastic tone,
"Would you mind if I put your bags in the trunk, or you got this?"
"Here!" I said with a bit of attitude.
I raised my polka dot luggage to show I'm strong,
and shoved them into him just a smidgen.
I can't tell you why I started freaking out in front of this fine man;
He was just doing his job driving me to the hotel!
All I know is that I needed to get to my room,
and bang my head on the wall in peace.
"Are you an art fan?"
Reggie asked me, while driving.
I thought,'Damn, he still wanted to hold a conversation with me.
Cute.
He was not checking for me.

Confidence; why do I do myself this way?
I just knew
I looked like a woman that's completely out of her comfort zone.
OKAY...breathe in goddess; breathe in.
Inhale; then a slow exhale...goddess breath.'
Then I retorted, "The 'LaPooh' sounded so swanky.
That was enough to peek my interest more."
"I am just a novice, who's interested in indulging."
"I like that attitude," said Reggie, in a somewhat sexy tone.
"I love art, for it can capture a single moment,
while telling a complete story without the narrative of words.
Everytime I gaze upon a painting; sculpture; tapestry---
hell, even furniture and tattoos---
I can appreciate the artists' desires,
I marvel in their creative complexity.
It's a privilege all of its own."
"That's why you're driving for an art gallery,
because you're a fan?"
"I love my job; and I love what I do.
I know being around books and quiet
all day would be rather boring, but it's so much more than that..."
Words escaped through my filter as I prepared to pardon
myself from the rest of our conversation.
"Could we please just go to the hotel?"
Reggie replied with a chuckle, "Wow; I like you."
Quickly, I had changed my mind about visiting 'The Gallery.'
Yet, I thought, 'What a disaster!'
'This guy probably thinks I'm a bitch!'
"No problem. Would you like to listen to the radio?"
Reggie asked politely, as he pulled away from, 'LaPooh's' entrance.
"Yes, please.
Put the radio station on whatever; it doesn't matter to me."
While in my head, I'm said, 'I need a drink.'
Reggie turned on the radio; "Again" by 'KDLPC' was playing.
Personally, I like, "Intoxicating Dance".
I couldn't believe he was singing one of my favorites!

Halfway through the song, we both are singing.
What is it about this guy;
or am I really all that horny right now?
Finally, after a few songs, we arrived at the hotel.
As soon as we pull up,
 the staff came and gave me first class service.
Opening the car door, Reggie offered me his hand.
As I took it to get out the car, the clasp on my bracelet broke.
I reached down to pick it up,
finding myself bumping heads with Reggie,
who apparently was being a gentleman,
trying to pick it up for me.
"Ouch!"
"I'm so sorry!"
"You're okay; great minds think alike," I told him.
From out of nowhere,
I kiss him on his cheek, and smell his cologne.
"Got to go!" I said with an embarrassing tone, and I leave.
I finally made it to my room.
I tipped the luggage person and closed the door.
I collapsed on--- a waterbed?
Damn; this is so 80s!
Well, if a swanky five-star hotel has them;
I guess they are making a comeback.
Combined with awkwardness and jet lag, I drift into a dream.
All I can tell you is that I am being painted by tattoo artists.
It is so erotic!
In this dream, I placed the artist's hand closer to my thighs.
I started feeling a vibration so good... waking up.
My phone!?
Thank you, Phone; as you vibrated near my thigh,
and I felt myself. I placed my cellphone to eye level,
and noticed a missed call from Tiff.

I had forgot to call her to tell her I made it.
After a twenty- minute shower, I called her on the video chat.
"Hey, girl! I'm sorry I didn't call earlier; that flight wore me out!"
"Don't worry about it..." replied Tiff.
"As long as you made it safely, we are all right."
"Yep, I'm here and as soon as I got here,
I embarrassed myself in front of this driver!"
I went on from there, and told her what happened.
I always know Tiff will give her words of wisdom.
"Go on, and get with him!
I put you some condoms in your cosmetics bag.
I them snuck in your luggage."
"What?" I am bewildered. "Yeah, girl.
I got skills.
When I dropped you off at the airport,
I placed some goodies in your suitcase.
You need to go shopping because your luggage is old;
and you should really change your combination!
You always use the same numbers."
"Hey, show me how the room looks."
"Tiff, I'm glad I love you, because you are something else,"
I said, getting up to grab the luggage.
"Hold on,"
"Oh, my!"
"That's what you packed in there, damn!"
Tiff replied, "I hooked you up with the VIP status at the store;
so you got the,'Feel Sexy' silk bras; thongs; body butter;
a pair of cute glitter stilettoes; gladiator sandals."
"A marijuana joint?!" I exclaimed.
"Tiffany! You had me smuggling drugs on a plane?!..."
"Chill out; it's just a joint!
You're not moving weight, or something like that."
Being silly, I told her that I couldn't find the lighter.
Tiff says, "Putting that in your bag would have been a big no-no."
We talked until I start getting hunger pains.
I told her I'll call her back.

Deciding to dine alone,

I ordered room service, and watched reality TV.

After watching two reunion shows,

I started thinking to myself that I do this shit at home.

Then I heard Tiff's voice say, 'Get up and be loose goosey!'

I put on some jeans, a tank top that says,

"Queen of English Literature" on it,

and put on the sandals from the bag.

I went for a walk, checking out the scenery and places close by.

Making my way back,

I entered the bar inside the hotel to get a book of matches,

plus a cherry-kiwi-orange daiquiri.

The bartender handed me my drink.

I turned and literally bumped into Reggie yet again.

"Are you stalking me!?"

I shyly exclaimed. "Hey!

You forgot to get your bracelet!

The one you dropped by the car.

I was going to drop it off at the front desk until now. Here you go."

"Hey, you fixed it! Thanks, Reggie; and it's shiny…"

"No problem; you have a good eye for jewelry.

Please; allow me get buy you another drink."

It's okay that he does,

even though my drink is still filled to the top.

Anyway.

"Oh! And, thank you!

It was my grandma's; she got it from her grandma,

so when she got sick she gave me and other

family members pieces of her jewelry before she passed."

"My condolences for your loss!

That is a beautiful piece she gave you."

"Thank you," I replied.

"Would you like a drink?

I would love to spend time with you," he said.

"What time are you picking me up?"

I have turned on my business mode voice.

Reggie smiled, "I'm not the regular driver;
I'm filling in for him. If you would like, I could be your escort?"
"No, thank you; but I will see you there, right?"
"No problem," Reggie said, with swagger.
He smiled at me and left. I thought to myself,
'I hate to see him go, but damn, he got a nice ass!
Mmm…where have my travels led me?'
I headed back to my room to complete my night.
I laid on the green ottoman, and fell asleep.
I must had been dreaming.
I watched this muscular figure gently painting my toenails purple.
I'm wearing an, "I Like Literature" tee shirt,
and before I can get further in the dream.
I'm awakened by my alarm playing, "Hey."
I opened and rolled my eyes in the back in my head, and
laid back down for a few more minutes.
The package deal was having brunch,
and going on a tour around the city.
I'm more interested in going to the gallery; but that's tomorrow.
I got up and got dressed.
I opened the door to room service of breakfast, and card.
It explained that I would be introduced to the other
winner of the contest.
After reading the correspondence,
I left and entered the dining area attached to the pool.
Before I can enjoy a taste of fruit from my plate, a voice
called out from the front entrance.
"Luci! I'm looking for Luci! Oh, there you are darling!"
It is a semi-athletic looking lady walking towards me.
"Hi!"
"Hello," I responded cautiously, and thought,
'Who in the hell is this chick?!'
She sits down and slowly crosses her legs,
as if to showcase her figure,
or maybe to entertain whomever cares to see?

"I'm Monica Jo; but you can call me 'Fern'."
She reached out to shake my hand.
"Fern?" I replied.
"Yep; I just love plants. Anyhoo.
I ran into that sexy man from the gallery...."
"Reggie?!"
I spewed out ever so quick as I shook her hand.
"Darling, yes! A sexy looking man!
He asked me to hand you this since we are tour buddies today!
We even got a personal driver that will arrive in forty minutes."
Fern handed me a note.
It said that he, 'apologized for not be the driver for today;
and that he was needed at the gallery.'
Funny enough, as she told me this, I began to blush.
At this point, I figured to talk as much as you want,
but my food was getting cold, and I am hungry!
It was something awkwardly cool about her though.
Ordering vodka and grapefruit juice,
she started talking about herself and business.
"I am the corporate manager of the, 'The Naughty Beauty,'
an adult novelty boutique."
"A sex store?! You wouldn't happen to know
a person by the name of Tiffany, do you?"
"No; who is she?" she asked.
"Never mind. Didn't some people get arrested
for breaking in there a while ago?" I asked.
"Sure, they did! I have a talent for reading people,
and even though I just met you,
there is something about your aura
that made my vibe tingle; and I liked it!
I never told anybody this, not even the police."
"But when I was watching the
store surveillance footage of smash and grabs.
It was a bike riding couple!"
"Honey, darling;
reviewing some of the footage was one hot scene!"
They were cleaning out the register,
took their time and everything."
"What!? Were they former employees; or something?!"
I exclaimed in an awkward, yet curious tone.

"I know, right!
Unfortunately, for legal reasons,
I can't say too much;but what I will tell you is that
they took their time not to rush...
like they had all the time in the world.
The couple started taking off each other's clothes.
The husband grabbed a couple of items off of various shelves.
That fucker started to rip open what appeared to be stockings,
placing them on his wife.
The entire act was like watching a romance movie!"
"He slid the stocking up to her thigh.
He made sure to caress her ankle as to feel
the silk on the tip of his fingers."
"Kissing her legs, he reached for a box and
placed some stilettos on her feet.
The misses took some furry handcuffs and
submissively laid across the counter.
The husband came back with a flogger,
and began lashing across her bottom.
With each stroke she dropped it low,
and positioned it back as if it tickled!"
"With each lash, I started getting aroused myself!
Once he finished,
she cuffed him and made him get on his knees.
Dinner was served!
I would have had him lick all in my ass!"
Fern stated and giggled.
Mmm; she looked as if she was having an orgasm.
While explaining, she started rubbing her breasts.
"Fern!"
It's like she got lost in the moment.
"Oh! I surely apologize;the things mature people can do."
Fern started fanning herself.
"Did you catch the thieves?"
"Yes," Fern said nonchalantly.
"This cop caught them coming out of the store,
and she charged them with vandalism, and for lewd acts of intimac
Oh, my, my, my!
I just can't get enough of...
Damn, I could just imagine it, a flashlight and handcuffs."
While Fern drifted in imagination, I was thinking to myself,
'I never found being in handcuffs and flogging sexy until for now.
As I take a sip of my coffee,the driver pulled up in a futuristic limc
with purple highlights.
" Right on schedule; let's go tear up the town!"

66

Obviously, Fern is an interesting person, whose approach is a more,
'in your face'.
While we were in the limo, I started to become more sociable with
her. The more stops we made, the more pubs we visited.
Even though she was allowing strangers
to do tequila shots off of her breasts, I admired
her personality more and more.
It was getting late, and we had to be
at the gallery tomorrow.
I spoke to Fern as she was tongue kissing the bartender.
"One moment; Luci!"
"I'll meet you in the limo; give me about five minutes,
eight at the max." Feeling too much of the alcohol, I said,
"Okay," and headed to the limo.
After a sobering minute,
I went back inside to make sure she was alright.
I couldn't see her at the bar, or on the dance floor,
but I noticed a line at the women's bathroom.
Several women were knocking on the door.
One lady yelled, "Damn! Bitch, fuck somewhere else;
I gotta piss!" I could only imagine she was talking about Fern!
"Go use the Men's! Uhh,, shit!"
Apologetic, I moved towards the door.
I said, "That's my sister," to curve any further incidents.
"Fern, it's Luci; are you alright?"
Moaning through the door, "Yes; my friend… ooh, shit; yes!"
"We gotta go. It's a long line out here and
someone might call the cops,
if no one did it already," I tried to reason with Fern.
"Fuck them! Ooh…uhh…oh…shit…!"
"I'm coming in!"
I yelled,
and rushed in.
Fern screamed.
As I entered the bathroom,
the bartender had Fern upside down in a split, eating her out.

"I always wanted to know how flexible I could get!"
The bartender gently placed her down.
"You're crazy!
Let's go," I replied, smiling.
As she was putting her clothes back on,
smiling was Fern's rebuttal.
Then she kissed the bartender,
and we started walking to the door.
A bunch of drunken fucks name called and threatened
to call the police.
Fern started laughing;
"Let's go back to the limo so we can go back to the hotel."
"You are a wild woman," I said to a parched Fern.
She was drinking bottled water from
the stocked limo fridge. Fern looked at me and said,
"We are on an expense paid vacation away;
with people we don't know. If we can't let our hair down
here, then what's the point of even trying to be adventurous?
Driver; to the hotel, please, and thank you!"
Other than listening to music, the drive was quiet.
Returning and walking towards the hotel doors, Fern said,
"Remember what I said about your aura?"
"Yes…" I spoke.
"You know why I said your aura makes me tingle?
It's because there's something about you that is just as
expressive as I am,but you just need the proper push."
Going in her purse, she grabbed something and said,
"Here."
"What's this?"
"My friend, this was my wedding ring.
I was married for five years;and on our fifth anniversary,
I came home to him having sex with his work-wife."
"OOOOOO…I exclaimed.

"I deserve to have fun!
 That was my push…
I wish yours to be fun and happy!
So tomorrow, find that push!"
Fern kisses me on the cheek.
"Goodnight, little sister." She goes to her room.
 Later that night, I kept tossing and turning,
replaying the scenes of the day.
Except, instead of Fern being the party,
it was me wearing nothing at all.
It felt so real that when I awakened my hand
was in my panties.
I'm tripping right now; I needed some fresh air.
While walking down my hotel floor's hallway,
I saw one of the emergency doors near the ice machine
slightly wedged opened by somebody's shoe.
Then I started hearing moaning noises from the other side.
Thinking to myself,
'Haven't I had enough adventure for one day?'
 I walked towards the door.
 Cautiously, I tried not to startle anyone.
Entering through the door that led to the emergency staircase,
I saw this couple was having sex on the stairs.
Part of me was thinking, 'Is Fern involved,
or she is going to find me down here watching!
 What is wrong with me?!'
I shouldn't be in to this; I mean watching this!
What if they caught me watching?
How embarrassing it
would be for all of us!
 But the way their bodies responded to each other is so sexy!
Getting more and more turned on, looking at every thrust,
I can't help but to finger myself a little… okay, a lot!
While watching,
I seldom glance over to make sure no one was around.
 As the couple began to climax in unison,
I left before they could notice. Back in my room,

I quickly jumped in the shower, and finished off my arousal.
Tomorrow had turned into today;
I'm extremely horny, with a slight hangover.
'Wow, what will today bring?'
I thought, as my phone rung.
It's the front desk telling me I have a phone call. It was Reggie!
"Hey; good morning!
I'm calling because the driver told me
about your wild night; are you alright?"
"Sure. Just a regular girls' night out," I said, nonchalantly.
"That's cool. I was wondering, would you like to have coffee?
I have some free time before the event..."
"Yes! Coffee, definitely!"
Just give me a moment, and I'm on my way down."
"I'll be here," replied. Reggie.
Rushing to freshen up,
I headed down to meet Reggie in the lobby.
"Hi, there." I said once I saw him.
With a look of delight, he replied,
"Thank you for having coffee with me! You will love this place."
"Really?" I said with a smile.
"Reggie, is this a date?"
"Well... I figured I would let you be the judge of that."
He smiled back.
Thinking in my head, 'Why did he just say that now, he looks even
more attractive.'
After we left the hotel, he took me to this really cool café
It had tons of poetic literature and art work.
We talked about various things:
sculptures; movies; books; music; etc.
He even recited a couple of poems.
He's a real renaissance type of guy, that's just so down to earth.
The two hours we spent seemed like a mere moment.
Upon bringing me back to the hotel,
I told him I would love for him to be my escort tonight.
"Uhh; about that. When you told me,
'No,' I volunteered for an "experience feast.'
I working with chefs', catering the affair."

"What do you do there?" I asked, with slight disappointment.
"It seems like everything,"
Reggie said with a smile; and gave me a hug.
In return, I kissed his lips with a sensual peck.
"Wow; we need to go out for coffee more often."
I smiled, "See you there." He winked and walked to his car.
The rest of the day, I got ready. I even hung out with Fern,
telling her what I saw last night.
"Girl, you should've texted me!
I would have loved to watch!"
When I mentioned to her about having coffee with Reggie,
she was excited.
"Why are you wasting time being shy?!"
"Get with him!"
"We're only here for a few more days."
"Crazy enough, my cousin said the same thing."
I turned to choose from the different outfits
Tiff picked for me to wear tonight.
Once I found the one, Fern helped me with my makeup,
and the transformation from homely to hotness began!
After the preparation was over,
Fern looked at me and said, "You are so beautiful!
Go on, girl!"
I even have Tiff via phone tell me to relax and have fun.
Finally, it was time to go to the art gallery.
As the limo picked us up, Fern asked, "Are you ready?"
"Let's do it!" I exclaimed as we proceeded to the limo.
When we got there, we were mesmerized by the atmosphere
lights and the sound; it was like an upscale electric circus.
The more we go down the corridors,
the more defined exotic and erotic sculptures we saw.

There was one sculpture in particular that caught my eye.
It was a living sculpture!
There were two people;and every sixty seconds they
posed in a different sex position.
My partner-in-crime was with me for most of the viewing,
until she saw a familiar face.
"Is that the bartender from that one pub?" I asked.
Fern pushed up her breasts and replied,
"Remembere what I told you? Have fun."
She walked towards the bartender's direction.
"Okay," I said to myself; all alone with no support system.
I had a little time, and
I found the others walking around 'The Gallery'.
I was not finding any more interesting art displays.
I saw tmore sculptures and paintings.
I even saw live art models, each more erotic than the last.
I walked towards the food.
What I found interesting were two people laying on a table.
The gallery visitors were eating various
fruits and cheeses off of their bodies.
I've never seen this before!
But it wasn't gross or embarrassing.
It looked quite tasteful.
As I approached closer,
I picked a few pieces of cheese off of the tray that was a guy.
Perhaps he checked out my hesitant manner,
because the guy started talking to me.
"Don't be shy! Nothing on me will bite you.
Of course; unless, you ask!"
"Please; forgive my husband.
He has a knack of making hoes feel special.
Not calling you one; of course."
I asked, "Is that how he got you?" She replied, "Bitch!
He had to work for this pussy! I'm a lady!"
"Please; forgive my wife; she had too much to drink."
"You would, too; if you were naked.People too close my pussy!"
 she exclaimed.
"Hi, I'm Leo.
This is my wife, Summer," Leo said.
We are the curators and part owners; we run it with my brother."

"Would his name happen to be Reggie?"
I asked.
"Why yes; you know him?"
I introduced myself.
Leo told me that Reggie mentioned me a couple of times.
I talked with them for a while.
 "Oh; my goodness!
How do you stay hard for so long?"
"Usually, I think of my wife," said Leo.
"When I'm mad at her, I think about her sister!"
"Just kidding; after people finish this tray,
someone else will be here.
We rotate."
Then Leo stated, "Hey, why don't you go to the kitchen?
Reggie should be here for the desert portion.
Just go through those double doors to your left,
and hang a right and you should see him."
"Are you sure?" I asked.
 "Definitely.
What my little brother gonna do; fire me?"
Taking Reggie's brother's open kitchen invite,
I walked towards the double doors, and turned left,
just to see another figure about the same size as Reggie.
I stopped and watched as this chef delicately
placed edibles on his body.
The only thing that is covered up is his face.
'Oh; how I would love to eat
that pineapple ring until I get to the bottom!'
I thought. The chef left,
I guess to get some more edible fruits and cheeses,
I walked closer to the beefcake of a tray.
I looked around just to make sure I won't get caught
as I worked up the nerve to grab something.
Okay; I'm going for it! Slowly,
I lowered my head to bob for pineapple rings,
until I got a creamy finish.
A voice said, "My brother said you were looking for me."
Being surprised, I scream.
The guy who I think is Reggie is startled; because he was asleep.
"You're alright, Luci?"
Reggie asked with a smirk.
"Fine; I'm fine."
Embarrassment loomed around the corner.

Reggie asked,
"So, when my brother told you where I would be,
and you saw the tray, did you think he was me?"
Thinking about the different adventures
I've been on since this trip,
I sent my embarrassment away.
I made sure when I looked in his eyes I told him.
"Yes."
"I was going to eat the entire thing,
because I thought that he was you."
Before Reggie could say anything,
I kissed him passionately, and held him;
letting him know that I've been yearning for him.
After sharing such a passionate, moist kiss,
he asked if I wanted to see his office,
and that it overlooked the city.
"Let's go," I began to blush.
We walked upstairs into his office,
and my body could not wait any more.
I practically ripped off his clothes
to get to his muscular flesh.
He started kissing me; touching my body.
I told him to rip my panties,
 and I wanted him inside me!
He picked me up and took me outside to the patio.
"Let's let the city see."
He placed me gently to my feet.
I embraced the side wall
as he placed himself inside of me.
Oh; if I could only scrapbook it!

La' Poohh

I saw you.

I met you.

I got to know you.

After a while; I knew I liked you.

Went on a couple dates.

Cool.

Intelligent; sexy; stylish.

The whole damn package.

May I unwrap it?

You know what I mean.

May I call you,

'My Queen La Poohh'? Simply,

you're the shit.

Damn, woman.

You know what I mean.

Looking just like your picture.

Then, I realized you truly.

Know What

The steam is exhausting, and refreshing
is the view of your silhouette.
Drawing back the shower curtain, undisputed;
until you stepped out, sexy and wet.
There are smells of fruit medley:
strawberries, and cherries;
moisturizing with shea butter.
Tastefully kissing your neck,
I sample your flavors with every sensual peck.
Whispering symphonic movements; passionately
conducting tongue linguistics;
and orchestrating sexually loquacious.
Illustration of narratives to intensify;
you and I practice in the most common of places.
Outside, on the side of the garage,
I unwrap you; my fondest of candies.
Nibbling from earlobes to nipples made of gumdrops;
with a bonbon bottom so high from a sugar rush.
I'm rock candy; you're marmalade;
let's get erotically stuck.
"What the f…?!"
"Hey, babe; there is an old couple looking at us;
across the street in the truck!"
Replying back, "Uhh; I don't care;
let them watch! Almost there… oh yeah, that's my spot!"
Surprised; but I'm not shocked.

Cool with me;
because I was mimicking the motion of the
sound of the bass that was beating down the block.
Bracing yourself on the garage,
you twist your wrist and lock.
Making music like, '
It-feels-so-good-I-don't-wanna stop!'
"Hold up; I mean, slow down!
I'm catching a cramp;
let's get on the hood of the car now."
Imagine a waterfall flowing nonstop.
"Now you're caramelized with Mr. Cherry on top."
You came when you creamed; ice cream drips
of sweat from what we've been doing for an hour.
"Don't that sound good;
I've been thinking about that...
just seeing you get out of the shower."

"What Had Happened"

Lying in bed, I open up one eye, after I feel someone turning over
A lady's arm drapes around my waist.
I think to himself, 'What the fuck what the hell just happened!?"
Okay, who is holding me?'
Turning over to see who the lady is, my mind starts working.
Remembering through an inebriated state of mind,
time starts moving slow, as I recall the events.
Starting the first day of my two weeks' vacation,
I woke to a knock at my door at 5:30 am.
Normally, I wouldn't even bother answering the door.
Except, on the other end was my next-door neighbor, Gina.
She is someone I know from back in the day.
We used to go to school together; but never really hung out much
When she told me about her moving,
I helped her box some of her things.
Looking out the peephole,
I see Gina has her hair pulled back, wearing a robe.
As I answer the door, Gina smiles, with slight embarrassment.
"I'm so sorry to bother you;
but I locked myself out of my apartment.
The leasing office doesn't open till ten,
and the movers will be here between eleven and twelve."
"How did you get locked out?" I ask.
"Well… I got up to put my carry-on bag in the car."
"Coming back, I realized I left my key in the apartment.
I'm locked out." "I'm not bothering you, am I?" ask Gina.
"I know it's so late; but it's early."
"No, no; you're fine; you're fine.
 Hold on; I need to put some pants on.
You're fine."
Curiosity intrigues; and my horn starts to show.
I open the door with much confidence.
"Come on in.
Would you like some coffee, or anything like that?"
"Coffee is fine, if you got a something to put in it," she smiles.
"Well, you know what today is? Your wish has been granted.

because I don't have to be at work."
"Lucky you," says Gina.
"After I move all my things to storage;
then return this rental car; pick up my tickets from the airport...
Oh; I didn't tell you?"
"I am the new head writer for two sitcoms in Australia."
I'll be flying to Arizona to spend the night with my cousin
until I leave the country."
"Moving out the country?
Wow, that's some big news! Congratulations! You inspire me."
"Really? Now would it be too much to ask you to do me a favor?"
"I thought the fact that you may want me naked was favor enough,"
I say on the sly.
"True; but I got a tiny favor to ask?"
"What?" I ask.
"When everything is done,
could you follow me as I return the rental car?"
"I need a ride to the airport; I would gladly appreciate it."
"Sure," I say in a hesitant matter.
As the coffeemaker brews,
I go in the kitchen to make a cup of coffee.
Gina sits up, removes the robe, and walks behind me.
She grabs my dick, and I stop in mid-motion.
"Even though I had an unfortunate mishap with the key,
and helping me was very nice of you,
I wanted to let you know that I liked
you back in the day; but I never thought I was your type.
Then when we became neighbors, I fantasized about the opportunity.
I figured with everything that's going on, why fucking fantasize?"
She lets me know what she clearly wants, but I am already aroused.
She starts off taking my off clothes.
The feeling is like a wave of erotic energy crashing
on our lustful emotions.
Craving each other's flesh, I pick her up and place her on my dick.
Amazed, and turned on more she says,
"I ...don't want....uh…shitI know I'm a little heavy…"
My response is placing her back to the wall,
making sure her leg was comfortable on my arms,
while my hands securely hold her.
My dick navigates inside her wetness,
thrusting and awakening her clitoris.

She is like, "Get this pussy!!!"
With every stroke, "Uhhh…shit...... right there ooh,
stay there! Fucking get this pussy!!!"
Even though her responses are still arousing,
my arms are beginning to cramp.
"Shit; your dick is deep in my pussy.
You gonna make me cum!!"
"Good!"
Even though she feels good, I have to set her down.
I want her to get hers; but after a while, my arms needed to rest.
I gently let her down to her feet, kissing her ever so sexy.
She has a slight drunken sway.
She takes my hand as we walk over to my couch.
She steps and places herself instantly in a position,
telling me how she wants me to satisfy her lustful pussy.
Damn!
She got a bad one; yes in deed!
Grabbing on my dick, pulling it towards her sensation.
Fuck! The way she is bouncing back is feeling so fucking good!
We keep going until we both cum.
After that, we laid on the couch, and fell asleep for a little bit.
Her phone starts to ring; it was her friend, Robin.
She is on her way to pick her up and take her to the airport.
 "Let's take a shower.
By the time Robin gets here,
we can get dirty and clean at the same time."
After the shower, she leaves.
As she walks back to her apartment, I ask,
"I thought you were locked out?"
"I lied," she says, giggling.
"I had the key in my pocket."
She goes into her place.

Probably no more than forty-five minutes pass.
I'm in jeans and a tee shirt, watching an old school movie,
when there was another knock at my door.
It is her again.
This time, she has someone with her.
"I don't want to bother you any further,
because you helped me a lot."
I think to myself,'You are definitely good for the bother.'
"Come in," I reply.
"Thanks! This is my girl, Robin.
I don't know if you remember her;
she graduated a year before us."
I extend my hand to Robin, but she gives me a hug.
"I remember you from being in the library."
"Ah, yeah, I remember now!
You would always take the book I was reading and close it."
"Yes, I did.
I apologize for that; I couldn't help but to mess with you," I reply.
Squeezing a little tighter she whispers,
"You smell good."
After the introductions and memory recollections,
we all sit and talk on the couch for a few minutes.
Then Gina says,"I hate to ask;
but could you help put the exercise equipment in the car?"
"Sure," I reply.
"Thank you; because I didn't want her to ask."
She's pointing at Robin.
"No problem; happy to; and I can take that truck back."
"You got to get to the airport," Robin states as she stands up.
"Hey! Thanks again!" Gina turns and looks at me.
"Wanna come to the airport to see me off?
Please?" she insists.
At this point, I'm already like it seems
my day has been inadvertently planned out.
As they bring out the luggage,
I put the exercise equipment in the rental truck.
I trail them to Robin's house to drop it off.
Then, they follow me to take the rental truck back,
with just in enough time to get Gina to the airport.

While there, the two friends go to the restroom.

I sit and watch a plane in mid-takeoff. I feel a hand on my head.

As I turn around and look up, it's my ex-girlfriend, Felicity.

"What the hell are you doing here?!"

I exclaim, as I stand to give her a hug.

"It's been forever! It's been seven years; are you married yet?"

"Naw," she replies, smiling. "What about you?"

"I was close; but it didn't work."

"Hey; I gotta go; but give me your number."

"My number; after seven years?" I ask.

Mischievously, she smiles and says,

"What; you don't want me to have it?"

"Whatever," I counter.

I give her the number.

"I'll call you." She gives me a hug and walks away.

Wow; what a fucking day this is turning out to be!

The friends come back and sit down.

Until Gina boards her flight, to pass time, we talk. That is cool.

I'm showing more attention to Robin,

"It was fun hanging out with y'all."

We are walking to the parking lot towards Robin's car.

"Yes; it was.

I never knew you were so cool," she blushes.

As we got in the car, she asks if I had to be anywhere.

My response is, "I'm on vacation."

She asks, "Could you help me assemble the exercise equipment?"

It's not because she can't do it herself;

she just wants an excuse to hang out longer.

Wow.

At this point,

I just had sex with her friend not too long ago,

and now she wants to hang out?

'Damn!' is what I am saying to myself!

"I'm not being a bother, am I?" she coos.

"No, no, not at all. It's cool you asked me."

"Really?"
Robin perks up.
"Really."
I smile.
We go back and forth with flirtatious rhetoric.
I am still thinking, 'What the hell I just got into?!'
We went back to her place to
put the exercise equipment together.
While listening to some R&B, Robin asks,
"Want a drink?"
"Yes; thank you!" I answer.
She comes back with a rare gin.
Robin mentions that she purchased it
during her vacation two years ago.
"I bought four bottles of this; consider yourself as
one of the lucky people to indulge in the last bottle."
"Goody," I say in a playful manner.
"Better said goody,
because this is smooth, and will have you on your ass."
"Let's do this, then."
"Alright, Macho; let's do it!".
She hands me one. I drink it, and damn it is delicious!
I give her a, 'This is tasty.' look.
She smiles, and pours some more.
"Shit! I know I'm gonna get hungry; what do you wanna eat?"
I ask. "It doesn't matter," she smiles.
I order two extra-large pizzas.
We start playing cards and, shit;
I'm really starting to feel the gin. "You're alright, darling?
It looks like the bottle got your attention," she purrs.
"Anyway; I'm good," I reply.
We take the entire evening to finish that bottle.
That gin got me feeling good!
"Robin, babe; where is the bathroom?"
I get up, feeling good and drunk.
"It's down the hall, and to the left."

Slightly stumbling, she gets up.
"Don't fall, sugar.
I'm too drunk to take you to the hospital."
Laughing, I reply, "I'm good.
I'm good." I walk towards the hallway.
As I open the door, this chick has a spa tub
in the middle of the big ass bathroom!
Damn; this nice!
I'm drunk, pissing, and looking at shit.
All of the sudden; the spa tub starts running!
She is right behind me.
I turn around.
"After you wash your hands;
can you help me get these boots off?"
says a topless Robin.
She sits on the edge of the spa tub.
After washing and drying my hands,
I forget to put my dick away.
She is just looking at me, with a grin.
I notice I am hanging out. Okay, honestly;
I wanted to see if I can get away with showing my dick.
"Come over here and help me," she states, smiling.
I'm not shit at this point; if you think about it;
I'm not with anyone…
Technically, I'm not being a whore I can live with that.
Splash!
As we unclothe and enter the spa's magical waters,
Robin's nibbles on my ear, whispering that she knows about my
morning fuck with her friend. She wants to find out for herself.
Grabbing condoms from a secret compartment,
she grabs my dick and puts on the condom. "Sit down."
Robin prepares to straddle me.
Just like her friend, both of them wanted me!
I guess I have been set up, or Robin just doesn't give a damn!!
Sex in a spa tub; wasted off gin…Alright! Robin is sexy as hell.

The way she is riding my dick, it's like she is lost in a trance.
"Damn; you in my pussy!
This is so fucking wild; I cannot believe this shit!"
"Damn; work this pussy!"
We keep going until we can't go no more.
I hang out with Robin until about eight.
Then, she takes me back home.
"Make sure you lock my number in your phone."
"Don't worry; I got you," I say, as I kiss her on the cheek.
As soon as I enter back in the apartment, Robin drives away.
Taking off my shoes and throwing them to the side,
I remove my clothes and get in the shower.
I start reminiscing on the acts of the day.
I started getting hard again.
Before I start to touch myself, my phone rings.
I try to ignore the phone. It rings again.
I get out the shower and answer it."Hey; you busy?"
"Naw," I reply, before asking,"Who's this?"
"Oh, you forgot me already?"
I am trying to get the voice right in my mind."It's Felicity, boy!
 What are you doing right now?"
"I just got home not too long ago."
She replies, "Hey; get dressed, and come with me! Me and my
girls, we got a party bus;and we're taking it to Kansas City."
Looking at the phone, I say to myself,'I'm doing it to myself.'
"Yeah. Come on; I'll get ready now."
"Cool! We are on our way…"

Blue Flame

Taste this kiss; moving in closer,
sensually licking your lips.
Feel that I'm stiff.
Embraced chest to tits.

Open your mouth a bit.
Having fun; mature as merlot.

The softest intertwine; your lips and mines.
Slow wine intoxicated;
caressing your hips; craving;
thirsting for more than just a sip.
Tongue in motion; expressing laid out lyrics,
literally, like this.
I'm lapping you, lady; lavishly,
loosely leaving you open.
Got your mind traveling at longitudes
and latitudes, on all levels. "Crème; you love it."
At this moment, my words, like your pussy,
are liquid as the ocean's head motions outside;
underneath a tree; looking and tasting so beautiful.
Clutching on the blanket used to rest;
your eyes roll back, and you don't know how to act.
You caress my hand,
as it moves up from your ankle to the thigh.
Grabbing my love, you place me inside.

As we listen to the artist Prince

while making love through a few of his greatest hits:

'Raspberry Beret';

'If I Was Your

Girlfriend';

'Darling Nikki';

'The Beautiful Ones';

with 'Pink Cashmere';

having 'Temptations';

'Let's Pretend We Are Married';

'Nothing Compares To U';

I 'Adore' U;

'Insatiable';

'Kiss';

'International Lover';

'Let's Go Crazy';

'When Doves Cry';

'Purple Rain';

'Soft & Wet';

'Under The Cherry Moon'.

Snuggle

I love you.
Hold and hug me tonight?
Kiss me goodnight,
while I'm awake?
Lighting the candles,
making a wish before
I drift asleep alongside a wishing well.
Your aura surrounds my spirit; inside of my shell,
I couldn't help but to look at myself.
You lifted?
I gazed up after I heard a shooting star cry and yell,
"What the hell!"
Chastised by Orion's Belt for being disrespectful,
grabbing a comet's tail.
Marveled in the scene,
my attention sits were inspiration dwells.
All I can see is a beautiful scheme
that I can tell in a literary theme.
As it seems that my third eye
isn't blind to the possibility of a living dream.

Message to Reader

No forget me nots; no roses.
Poor romance
inside a crowded club.
No one speaks of love;
but lust is still popping in the velvet tub
with no cares.
I got love for sale; not the physical.
but the emotion itself.
I got the finest elixir you can't get nowhere else.

Welcome to my passion factory.
Romantic humor, and messy lighthearted drama.

Indulge in literature and art!

Author: Peter Cherry

A Saint Louis, MO native, he is an author,
songwriter; producer, publisher, artist,
and a Co-founder of the musical group; "KDLPC"
with Kalisha D. Lemmitt-Cherry.
He established "Angelic Reign, Inc."
publishing company in 2004.
Peter has obtained: Associates Degree in Communications
(St. Louis Community College at Florissant Valley);
Bachelor of Science in Media Studies
(University of Missouri Saint Louis)
Master of Arts in Counseling
(Lindenwood University).

Angelic Reign Presents

EP SOUNDTRACK

Prunus Serotina

(Black Cherries)

Erotic Tales

By Peter Cherry

Angelic Reign Inc.

PARENTAL
ADVISORY
EXPLICIT CONTENT

The Music Soundtrack

'KDLPC' is
Kalisha D. Lemmitt-Cherry and Peter Cherry

Music Singles

Truly Love

Per La Mae

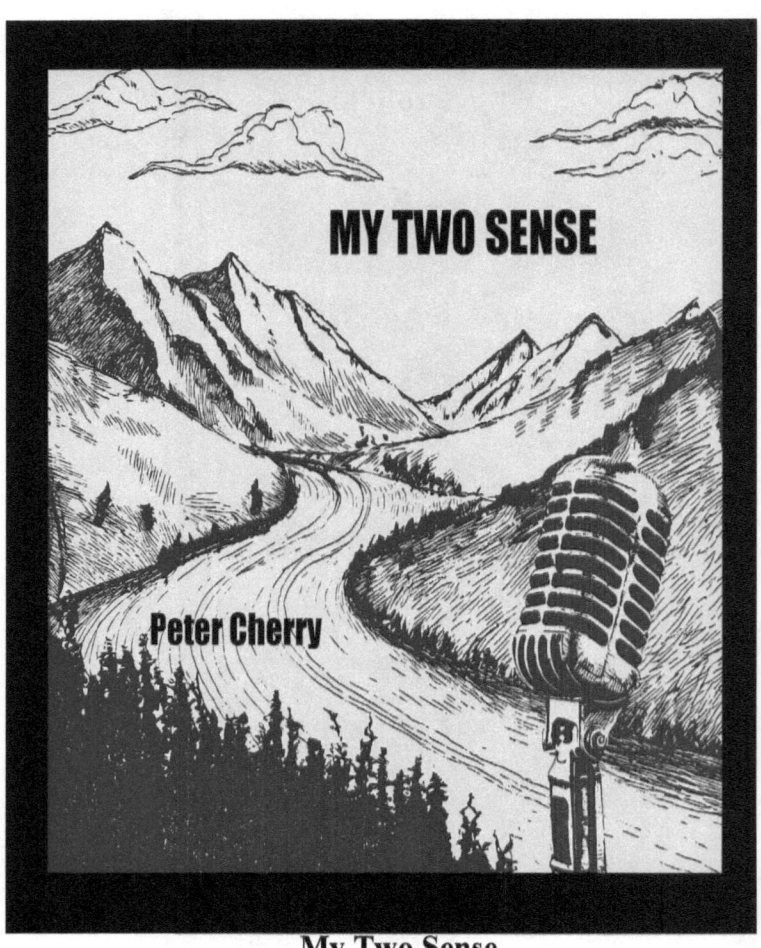

My Two Sense

The Music Soundtrack